JUNIOR BIOS

Joe Biden

BY KATE MIKOLEY

Please visit our website, www.enslow.com. For a free color catalog of all our high-quality books, call toll free 1-800-398-2504 or fax 1-877-980-4454.

Library of Congress Cataloging-in-Publication Data

Names: Mikoley, Kate, author.
Title: Joe Biden / Kate Mikoley.
Description: New York : Enslow Publishing, [2021] | Series: Junior bios | Includes bibliographical references and index.
Identifiers: LCCN 2021000272 | ISBN 9781978525900 (library binding) | ISBN 9781978525887 (paperback) | ISBN 9781978525894 (6 pack) | ISBN 9781978525917 (ebook)
Subjects: LCSH: Biden, Joseph R., Jr.–Juvenile literature. | Presidents–United States–Juvenile literature. | Politicians–United States–Biography–Juvenile literature. | United States–Politics and government–2017–Juvenile literature. | United States. Congress. Senate–Biography–Juvenile literature. | United States–Politics and government–1989–Juvenile literature. | Delaware–Biography–Juvenile literature.
Classification: LCC E840.8.B54 M55 2021 | DDC 973.934092 [B]–dc23
LC record available at https://lccn.loc.gov/2021000272

First Edition

Published in 2021 by
Enslow Publishing
101 West 23rd Street, Suite #240
New York, NY 10011

Copyright © 2021 Enslow Publishing

Designer: Deanna Paternostro
Editor: Kate Mikoley

Photo credits: Cover, pp. 1 (Joe Biden), 5 Stratos Brilakis/Shutterstock.com; cover, p. 1 (photo frame) Aleksandr Andrushkiv/Shutterstock.com; marble texture used throughout HardtIllustrations/Shutterstock.com; lined paper texture used throughout Mtsaride/Shutterstock.com; watercolor texture used throughout solarbird/Shutterstock.com; p. 6 (inset), 7 RCHIVIO GBB/Alamy Stock Photo; p. 9 Image Press Agency/Alamy Stock Photo; p. 11 REUTERS/Alamy Stock Photo; p. 13 ZUMA Press, Inc./Alamy Stock Photo; pp. 15, 19 UPI/Alamy Stock Photo; p. 17 White House Photo/Alamy Stock Photo.

All rights reserved. No part of this book may be reproduced in any form without permission in writing from the publisher, except by a reviewer.

Printed in the United States of America

CPSIA compliance information: Batch #BSENS22: For further information contact Enslow Publishing, New York, New York, at 1-800-542-2595.

Find us on

Contents

A Political Leader 4
Early Life 6
Political Beginnings 8
A Win Followed by Loss 10
Serving on the Senate 12
Second in Command 14
Race to the White House 18
Joe's Timeline 21
Glossary 22
For More Information 23
Index 24

Words in the glossary appear in **bold** type the first time they are used in the text.

A Political Leader

In 2009, Joe Biden became the 47th vice president of the United States. He served as President Barack Obama's vice president for two terms. In 2020, Joe ran for president himself. That November, he won the election, securing his place as the next president of the United States. Joe's political career, however, started well before his days working in the White House.

Joe's early career included many accomplishments, but this time in his life also came with hardship. Read on to learn how Joe Biden went from being a kid in Pennsylvania to holding the highest office in the United States.

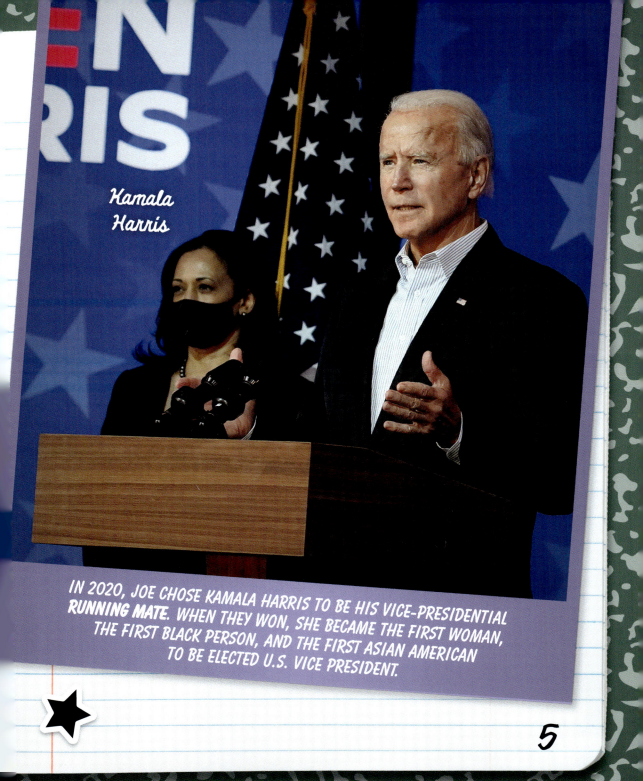

Kamala Harris

In 2020, Joe chose Kamala Harris to be his vice-presidential **running mate**. When they won, she became the first woman, the first Black person, and the first Asian American to be elected U.S. vice president.

Early Life

Joe was born in Scranton, Pennsylvania, on November 20, 1942, to Joseph Robinette Biden Sr. and Catherine Eugenia Finnegan Biden. Joe's full name is Joseph Robinette Biden Jr., after his father. He is the oldest of four siblings. In 1953, the Biden family moved to Claymont, Delaware, in New Castle County, where his father worked selling used cars.

FACTS BEHIND THE FIGURE

When Joe was a kid, he spoke with a stutter. As an adult, he still stutters sometimes. People made fun of his stutter in school, but he worked hard to become a good public speaker. Joe has said that his stutter helped him learn *empathy*.

JOE'S FIRST RUN FOR PRESIDENCY WAS IN HIGH SCHOOL! HE WAS CLASS PRESIDENT IN BOTH HIS JUNIOR AND SENIOR YEARS AT ARCHMERE ACADEMY.

After high school, Joe went to the University of Delaware. He studied history and political science and graduated in 1965. In 1966, Joe married Neilia Hunter. The couple later had two sons, Beau and Hunter, and a daughter named Naomi.

Political Beginnings

After graduating from the University of Delaware, Joe went on to study law at Syracuse University in New York. He graduated from there in 1968. Then, he moved back to Delaware and began working as a lawyer.

It wasn't long before Joe's career turned to politics. He ran for New Castle County Council and won the election by 2,000 votes. He served on the council from 1970 to 1972. In 1972, he ran to become one of the U.S. senators from Delaware. When he won—at age 29—he became one of the youngest people ever elected to the U.S. Senate.

Valerie Biden Owens

JOE'S SISTER, VALERIE, WAS HIS CAMPAIGN MANAGER IN THE 1972 ELECTION. SHE HAS SINCE WORKED WITH HIM ON MANY OTHER CAMPAIGNS.

The U.S. Constitution states that members of the Senate must be at least 30 years old. Although Joe was only 29 when elected senator, he turned 30 before taking office.

A Win Followed by Loss

About a month after winning his first U.S. Senate election, Joe was faced with **tragedy**. His wife, Neilia, and baby daughter, Naomi, died in a car accident. Beau and Hunter were in the car too. They survived the accident but were seriously hurt.

FACTS BEHIND THE FIGURE

When he first became a senator, Joe would drive to work from Delaware to Washington, D.C. It was a long drive, but this way he could still see his sons in the morning and evening. He later started making the daily journey by train.

JOE IS KNOWN FOR HIS LOVE OF TRAVELING BY TRAIN. EVEN WHEN HIS SONS GOT OLDER, HE CONTINUED TAKING THE TRAIN TO WORK IN WASHINGTON THROUGHOUT HIS WHOLE CAREER IN THE SENATE.

At first, Joe thought about stepping away from his political career. However, in the end, he decided to take the position he was elected to. Joe officially became a U.S. senator in 1973. He was sworn in at the hospital where his sons were staying, right beside their beds.

Serving on the Senate

Joe was reelected to the Senate six times, serving for 36 years. This made him Delaware's longest-serving U.S. senator and put him among the longest-serving U.S. senators in the country.

Joe's Senate work dealt with issues such as drug **policy**, criminal justice, and relations between the United States and other countries. Another key issue he worked on was addressing **climate change**. He introduced a bill in 1986 that is thought to be one of the first climate change bills introduced to Congress. Joe was also part of the Senate's Committee on the Judiciary, a group that oversees the Department of Justice, for many years.

Dr. Jill Biden

JILL STARTED TEACHING AT NORTHERN VIRGINIA COMMUNITY COLLEGE IN 2009. SHE OFTEN SPEAKS ABOUT THE IMPORTANCE OF COMMUNITY COLLEGES.

FACTS BEHIND THE FIGURE

In 1977, Joe married his second wife, Jill Jacobs. A few years later, they had a daughter, Ashley. Jill has a **doctorate** in education and has taught English at both high school and college levels.

13

Second in Command

In 1988 and 2008, Joe sought to be **nominated** by the Democratic Party to run for president. He ended up dropping out of the race both times.

In 2008, Barack Obama won the Democratic Party's nomination. He chose Joe to be his vice-presidential running mate. This meant that if Barack became president, Joe would be his vice president—and that's exactly what happened! On November 4, 2008, Barack Obama and Joe Biden won the election. Joe also won reelection for his Senate seat but gave up that position before taking office as vice president.

JOE WAS SWORN IN AND OFFICIALLY BECAME VICE PRESIDENT ON JANUARY 20, 2009.

In His Own Words
"We have to lead not just by the example of our power, but by the power of our example."

15

After being reelected in 2012, Barack and Joe served a second term as president and vice president. In total, Joe was vice president for eight years. During this time, he accomplished a lot. Joe used his experience working with other countries to advise the president on **international** matters.

FACTS BEHIND THE FIGURE

Sadly, Joe's son Beau died of brain cancer in 2015. In 2017, Joe came out with a book called *Promise Me, Dad: A Year of Hope, Hardship, and Purpose*. The book talks about the loss of his son and other events around that time.

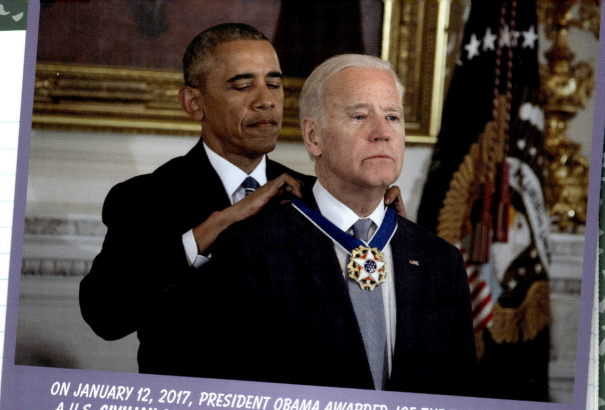

ON JANUARY 12, 2017, PRESIDENT OBAMA AWARDED JOE THE TOP HONOR A U.S. **CIVILIAN** CAN RECEIVE—THE PRESIDENTIAL MEDAL OF FREEDOM. THIS IS GIVEN TO PEOPLE WHO HAVE MADE IMPORTANT CONTRIBUTIONS TO THE COUNTRY OR WORLD.

Joe also played an important part in rebuilding the U.S. economy after a serious financial **crisis** happened in 2007 and 2008. He helped to pass and carry out the American Recovery and Reinvestment Act, a plan to help the economy get better. The act also dealt with clean energy.

Race to the White House

Toward the end of Joe's second term as vice president, people started wondering if he would run for president in 2016. However, he eventually said that he would not do so, as he and his family were dealing with the loss of Beau.

In His Own Words
"We were born of an idea, that every single solitary person, given half a chance, no matter where they're from, given half a chance, there is not a single thing they cannot do if they work at it. Nothing is beyond their *capacity*."

THE PRESIDENTIAL ELECTION BETWEEN DONALD TRUMP AND JOE BIDEN WAS HELD ON NOVEMBER 3, 2020. COUNTING THE VOTES TOOK LONGER THAN USUAL, BUT IN THE END, JOE WON.

However, in 2019, Joe joined many Democrats in a fight for the party's presidential nomination. In the end, Joe won the nomination and became the 2020 Democratic candidate for president. His campaign dealt with many issues, such as fighting climate change, creating jobs and helping people with low incomes, and expanding federal health care.

The 2020 election was unlike any other in history. It happened during the **COVID-19 pandemic**. Still, more people voted in 2020 than in any other year since 1900. Many voted by mail.

It's common for election results to be publicly known by the next day. However, because of the pandemic and the high number of mail-in **ballots**, counting the votes took longer than usual. Four days after the election, on November 7, enough votes were counted to make it clear that Joe had won. He was sworn into office and his presidency officially began on January 20, 2021.

Joe's Timeline

1942: Joe is born on November 20.

1965: Joe graduates from the University of Delaware.

1966: Joe marries Neilia Hunter.

1968: Joe graduates with a law degree from Syracuse University.

1970: Joe begins serving on the New Castle County Council.

1972: Joe is elected to the U.S. Senate. About a month later, his wife and daughter die in a car accident.

1977: Joe marries Jill Jacobs.

1988: For the first time, Joe runs for the Democratic Party's presidential nomination.

2008: Joe seeks the Democratic nomination again. Barack Obama selects him as his vice-presidential running mate.

2009: Joe becomes vice president on January 20.

2012: Joe is reelected vice president.

2020: Joe wins the Democratic nomination for president and wins the election held on November 3.

2021: Joe takes office as president of the United States on January 20.

21

Glossary

ballot A sheet of paper listing candidates' names and used for voting.

capacity The ability to do or experience something.

civilian A person not on active duty in the military.

climate change Long-term change in Earth's climate, caused partly by human activities such as burning oil and natural gas.

COVID-19 pandemic A time during which COVID-19, a disease caused by a coronavirus, spread very quickly and affected a large number of people throughout the world.

crisis A difficult or unsafe situation that needs attention or help.

doctorate The highest degree offered by a university. It requires many years of study.

empathy The understanding and sharing of another person's emotions and experiences.

international Involving two or more countries.

nominate To suggest someone for an honor or office.

policy A plan of general and future decisions and positions.

running mate A person who runs with someone in an election and who is given the lower position if elected. Usually refers to a person running for vice president.

tragedy A terrible accident.

For More Information

Books
Rose, Rachel. *President Joe Biden: America's 46th President*. Minneapolis, MN: Bearport Publishing Company, 2021.

Thomas, Rachel L. *Joe Biden*. Minneapolis, MN: Abdo Publishing, 2021.

Websites
Joe Biden
www.history.com/topics/us-politics/joe-biden
Learn more about Joe's life and career here.

Joe's Story
joebiden.com/joes-story/
Read more about Joe's life on his official campaign website.

Publisher's note to educators and parents: Our editors have carefully reviewed these websites to ensure that they are suitable for students. Many websites change frequently, however, and we cannot guarantee that a site's future contents will continue to meet our high standards of quality and educational value. Be advised that students should be closely supervised whenever they access the internet.

Index

Biden, Ashley, 13

Biden, Beau, 7, 10, 16, 18

Biden, Hunter, 7, 10

Biden, Dr. Jill Jacobs, 13, 21

Biden, Naomi, 7, 10

Biden, Neilia Hunter, 7, 10, 21

climate change, 12, 19

Constitution, U.S., 9

COVID-19, 20

Harris, Kamala, 5

New Castle County Council, 8, 21

Obama, Barack, 4, 14, 16, 17, 21

Owens, Valerie Biden, 9

Senate, U.S., 8, 9, 10, 11, 12, 14, 21

Syracuse University, 8, 21

University of Delaware, 7, 8, 21